# BREAKOUT at the BUG LAB

by Ruth Horowitz
pictures by Joan Holub

PUFFIN BOOKS

D0028844

*To Trish, my favorite entomologist*
R.H.

*For Cecile Goyette and Kimi Weart, with many thanks*
J.H.

PUFFIN BOOKS
Published by the Penguin Group
Penguin Putnam Books for Young Readers, 345 Hudson Street, New York, New York 10014, U.S.A.
Penguin Books Ltd, 80 Strand, London WC2R ORL, England
Penguin Books Australia Ltd, Ringwood, Victoria, Australia
Penguin Books Canada Ltd, 10 Alcorn Avenue, Toronto, Ontario, Canada M4V 3B2
Penguin Books (N.Z.) Ltd, 182-190 Wairau Road, Auckland 10, New Zealand
Penguin Books Ltd, Registered Offices: Harmondsworth, Middlesex, England

First published in the United States of America by Dial Books for Young Readers,
a division of Penguin Putnam Inc., 2001
Published by Puffin Books, a division of Penguin Putnam Books for Young Readers, 2002

9  10  8

THE LIBRARY OF CONGRESS HAS CATALOGUED THE DIAL EDITION AS FOLLOWS:
Horowitz, Ruth.
Breakout at the bug lab/by Ruth Horowitz;
Pictures by Joan Holub—1st ed.
p.  cm.
Summary: When a giant cockroach named Max escapes from their mother's bug laboratory,
Leo and his brother receive help from a mysterious stranger who advises
them to think like a bug in order to recapture the runaway roach.
ISBN 0-8037-2510-8
[1. Cockroaches—Fiction. 2. Insects—Fiction. 3. Brothers—Fiction.] I. Holub, Joan, ill. II. Title.
PZ7.H7877Br  2001
[Fic]—dc21  99-14274  CIP
*The art was created using watercolor, gouache, and acrylic paints on Arches watercolor paper.*

Puffin Easy-to-Read ISBN 0-14-230200-7
Puffin® and Easy-to-Read® are registered trademarks of Penguin Putnam Inc.

Printed in China

Reading Level 2.1

# CONTENTS

# MOM'S BUG LAB

Our mom works in a bug lab.

She collects robber flies.

They carry their food with their feet.

She looks at dung beetles.

They eat animal poop!

But the best bug in her lab is Max.

Max is Mom's pet cockroach.

Max comes from an island near Africa.

He loves fruit and hates bright lights.

Max is as big as a bite-sized candy bar.

He hisses like a snake when he is mad.

Mom keeps Max in a glass tank.

She feeds him dog food

and banana peels.

She puts a board over the tank.

It keeps Max from climbing out.

Max is not like most pets.

When most people see him,

they do not talk baby talk.

They do not try to pat him.

Mostly they back away.

Sometimes they scream.

But Mom loves Max,

and so do Leo and I.

The bug lab is in a long glass building
with many other kinds of labs.
The people who work there help keep
our air, water, fish, and plants healthy.

One day Mom told us that

the building was getting a new name—

The Ruby L. Gold Nature Center.

"Ruby L. Gold is a lady who

loves nature, even bugs," Mom said.

The day the building got its new name

was the day Max broke out.

A big party was planned for the new name.

There would be TV cameras.

Some big shots would make speeches.

And Ruby L. Gold would cut a red ribbon.

Please come to a party
for the new
RUBY L. GOLD
NATURE CENTER

1630 Ripton Road
June 19th at 11 a.m.
R.S.V.P.

Mom wanted us to look nice for the party.

Leo and I had to wear white shirts.

We had to wear bright ties.

They were too itchy and too tight.

Mom got a haircut.

It made her look kind of like a poodle.

On the way to the lab, Mom told us,

"Do not make faces at the TV cameras.

Do not make noises during the speeches.

And do not do anything at all

around Ruby L. Gold."

"We will be good," I promised.

"As good as gold," added Leo.

# MAX ON THE LOOSE!

When we got to the lab,

we did what we always do.

Mom took the board off Max's tank.

I put dog food into his dish.

Leo put the board back.

Next, Mom showed us her neat new bugs.

There was a jar of wiggly worms

and a bag of gold beetles.

There was a box of fat white grubs.

"Want to take a closer look

at these grubs?" Mom asked.

"Sure!" we said. Up close, we could see

their big heads and fat mouths.

We could see food moving inside them.

"Yuck!" Leo grinned.

While we watched the grubs,

Mom had to leave for a meeting.

"Come to the party in half an hour.

And don't forget the rules," she said.

"We will be good," I promised.

"We will not bug anyone," added Leo.

Mom left the lab and we went to see

if Max had eaten his food.

The board was out of place.

The dog food was gone.

And so was Max!

We hunted for Max behind the grubs.

We searched beside the robber flies.

We even checked under the dung beetles.

I looked high. Leo looked low.

We covered every inch of that lab.

There was not a roach in sight.

Max was on the loose!

"Oh, no!" Leo groaned.

"There will be TV cameras.

There will be big shots making speeches.

And there will be Ruby L. Gold herself!

If they see Max, they will all scream.

Ruby L. Gold will run away.

And Mom will be mad as a hornet!"

"You're right," I said. "We must find Max

before anyone else does!"

First we looked in the plant lab.

We saw flowers as fat as our heads.

There was no giant cockroach.

Then we searched in the fish lab.

I found a fish that looked like Leo.

But we did not find Max.

Next we hunted in the air lab.

There were big buzzing machines.

There were no big hissing bugs.

We even checked the bathroom.

I searched in the sink.

Leo looked in the toilet.

Max was not in either one.

"He is not on this floor," said Leo.

We ran to the stairs.

"Aha!" I shouted. There was Max.

He was hanging by his feet like a bat.

We jumped and jumped.

But Max was too high to reach.

"Climb up on top of me," I told Leo.

"Ouch!" I yelled as Leo pulled my hair.

But he still could not reach Max.

"I have an idea," said Leo.

We found a broom in Mom's lab.

Leo climbed onto my back.

He held the broom over his head.

I jumped and jumped.

It was a neat trick. It made me dizzy.

But it did not bring Max down.

# ONE-SHOT LIL

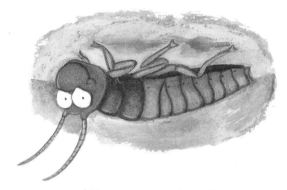

Leo was still on my back

when we heard someone clapping.

I turned us around and saw a lady.

She had twinkling eyes and she

was grinning a crooked grin.

"That is a neat trick," the lady said.

Then she looked up and saw Max.

We put our hands over our ears.

We waited for the scream.

The lady did not scream.

But she did talk very loudly.

"I JUST LOVE BATS!" she yelled.

We took our hands off our ears.

Leo climbed down off of me.

"That's not a bat," I told the lady.

"That's Max, our pet cockroach.

If we do not get him down,

the TV cameras will see him.

The big shots will scream.

Ruby L. Gold will run away.

And Mom will be as angry as a fire ant."

"Then we *must* get him down," she said.

"But we tried," Leo told her.

"Well," said the lady, "to make a roach

do what you want,

maybe you need to *think* like a roach."

We all started thinking.

"What does Max love?" the lady asked.

"Fruit and dog food!" I shouted.

"Good," said the lady.

We found both in the bug lab.

I put dog food on a banana peel.

The lady put the peel on the broom.

Leo climbed back onto me.

The lady handed him the broom.

He held it up high for Max to smell.

But Max did not move.

"He just ate," I told the lady.

"Maybe he's not hungry."

Just then, the banana peel slipped.

The slimy mess plopped on Leo's head.

"Double yuck!" Leo yelled.

"We need a new plan," said the lady.

"I know. What does Max hate?"

"Bright lights," said Leo.

"Okay then." The lady smiled.

"I have just the thing."

And she did!

She took a small light from her purse.

She pushed a button.

She pointed the light at Max.

Max ran away from the light.

He hid behind the smoke alarm.

"Holy smokes!" cried Leo.

We thought some more.

At last the lady said, "There is only

one thing left to do.

"Can you find some rubber bands?"

Leo and I found rubber bands

in the lab.

We stuffed them into our pockets.

We ran back to the stairs.

The lady took a rubber band.

She looped one end over her finger.

She pulled the other around her thumb.

"I have not done this in years," she said.

"But when I was your age,

my aim was so good,

the kids called me One-Shot Lil."

One-Shot Lil was going to shoot Max!

"Stop!" I cried. "You might hurt him!"

"Don't worry," said One-Shot.

"I am not going to hit him. But if I did,

his hard shell would keep him safe."

One-Shot pointed her finger at Max.

"Get ready!" she shouted.

*Zing!* The rubber band flew.

*Ping!* It hit the alarm.

And that *PING* shook Max loose.

I put my hands out and caught Max,

just like a pop fly.

"Good catch!" said One-Shot.

"Great shot!" Leo cheered.

Max grabbed my thumb.

I put my other hand over him.

"Thanks for helping," I told One-Shot.

"And for not screaming," Leo added.

One-Shot grinned.

"See you at the party!"

# BUG-EYED AT THE PARTY

We took Max back to Mom's lab.

I set Max down in his tank.

I put the board on top.

Leo put a big book on the board.

I put a dog food can on the book.

Leo put a rock on the can.

We told Max, "Stay!"

Then we went to the party.

The room was bright with TV lights.

It was full of TV cameras.

Everyone clapped as we walked in.

Leo bowed. "Thank you, thank you!"

I poked him in the ribs.

"The clapping is not for us," I told him.

A big shot got up on the stage.

He gave a speech. Leo burped in my ear.

Mom poked him in the ribs.

When the big shot was finally done,

a new big shot got up.

She gave a speech.

Leo made a rubber band go *twang*.

Mom took it away.

When the speech was over,

Leo poked me in the ribs.

He pointed to the stage.

There was One-Shot Lil,

grinning her crooked grin at the crowd.

"What is she doing up there?" I asked.

"Shh!" said Mom, poking me.

One-Shot was speaking to the crowd.

"This center does good work,"

she said, "for air and water.

It does good work for fish and plants,

and even bugs.

Thank you for all you do.

Now, let's have a fun party."

Then One-Shot cut the red ribbon.

"I thought Ruby L. Gold

was going to do that," Leo said.

"She just did," Mom told him.

"Now stop staring, you two.

You look all bug-eyed."

After she cut the ribbon,

One-Shot L. Gold looked at the labs.

The TV people came too.

When she got to the bug lab,

One-Shot went up to Max's tank.

"A giant hissing cockroach!"

she cried. "May I hold him?"

"Of course, Ms. Gold," said Mom.

"Call me One-Shot," said our friend.

Mom did not say anything.

She just looked all bug-eyed.

That night, Mom and Max, Leo and I,

and One-Shot L. Gold

were on the TV news.

One-Shot was holding Max.

Leo was poking me in the ribs.

Mom looked kind of like a poodle.

"Thanks for being so good at the party,"

Mom said when the news was over.

"I am glad you met Ruby L. Gold.

She is a very smart lady.

But why is she called One-Shot?"

"Beats me," I said.

Leo just grinned a crooked grin.

Then he reached into his pocket

and shot a rubber band at the ceiling.